First published in 2000 by
Franklin Watts
338 Euston Road
London
NW1 3BH

Franklin Watts Australia
Level 17 / 207 Kent Street
Sydney
NSW 2000

A CIP catalogue record for this book is available
from the British Library.

ISBN 978 0 7496 4388 1

Series Editor: Louise John
Series Advisor: Dr Barrie Wade
Series Designer: Jason Anscomb

Printed in China

Franklin Watts is a division of
Hachette Children's Books
an Hachette Livre UK company.

Recycled!

by Jillian Powell

Illustrated by Amanda Wood

FRANKLIN WATTS
LONDON•SYDNEY

Class 2d was learning all about recycling.

"Let's start a recycling bank," said Miss Drew.

"We can put it in the school hall."

Some people brought bottles
Some people brought cans.

Others brought newspapers,
egg boxes or old clothes.

Soon, the recycling bank
was almost full.

"Next week we'll take it to the recycling centre in town," said Miss Drew.

Miss Han was the art teacher.

Next day at Assembly,
she saw all the egg boxes.

"We'll use them to make an alligator," she told Miss Drew

So she took them back to
her classroom.

Mrs Bell, the dinner lady,
saw all the bottles
and jars.

"I'll use these for my jam,"
she told Miss Drew.

So, she took them home
and made lots of jam.

Mr Timms, the headmaster, was moving house.

He needed something to
wrap his china in.

"These newspapers are just what I need," he told Miss Drew.

So he used them to wrap
up his china.

Mr Green, the caretaker,
saw the tin cans.

"I know what I can do with these," he told Miss Drew.

Mrs Roberts, the RE teacher, saw the old, woollen clothes.

"These are just what I need,"
she told Miss Drew.

When 2d came to collect
the rubbish, it had all gone.

"It's all been recycled!" said Miss Drew.

So they started recycling
all over again!

31

Leapfrog has been specially designed to fit the requirements of the Literacy Framework. It offers real books for beginning readers by top authors and illustrators. There are 67 Leapfrog stories to choose from:

* hardback